TRADITIONAL STORIES OF THE GREAT BASIN AND PLATEAU NATIONS

BY CARLA MOONEY

CONTENT CONSULTANT
Larry Cesspooch
Ute Filmmaker and Storyteller
Through Native Eyes Productions

Core Library

An Imprint of Abdo Publishing
abdopublishing.com

Cover image: A Shoshone-Bannock man poses wearing traditional clothing.

abdopublishing.com

Published by Abdo Publishing, a division of ABDO, PO Box 398166, Minneapolis, Minnesota 55439. Copyright © 2018 by Abdo Consulting Group, Inc. International copyrights reserved in all countries. No part of this book may be reproduced in any form without written permission from the publisher. Core Library™ is a trademark and logo of Abdo Publishing.

Printed in the United States of America, North Mankato, Minnesota
042017
092017

Cover Photo: Marilyn Angel Wynn/NativeStock
Interior Photos: Marilyn Angel Wynn/NativeStock, 1; Dominique Taylor/Vail Daily/AP Images, 4–5; Red Line Editorial, 6; iStockphoto, 8–9, 12–13, 26–27, 30, 43; B. Anthony Stewart/National Geographic/Getty Images, 10; Gordon King/Yakima Herald-Republic/AP Images, 18–19, 45; Bill Schaefer/Getty Images News/Getty Images, 21; Tony Campbell/Shutterstock Images, 22 (top); Shutterstock Images, 22 (right); Insect World/Shutterstock Images, 22 (bottom); Dave Alan/iStockphoto, 22 (left); Peter Turnley/Corbis Historical/VCG/Getty Images, 34–35; Eileen Kovchok/AP Images, 38; Mark Ralston/AFP/Getty Images, 40

Editor: Arnold Ringstad
Imprint Designer: Maggie Villaume
Series Design Direction: Ryan Gale

Publisher's Cataloging-in-Publication Data

Names: Mooney, Carla, author.
Title: Traditional stories of the Great Basin and Plateau nations / by Carla Mooney.
Description: Minneapolis, MN : Abdo Publishing, 2018. | Series: Native American oral histories | Includes bibliographical references and index.
Identifiers: LCCN 2017930247 | ISBN 9781532111723 (lib. bdg.) | ISBN 9781680789577 (ebook)
Subjects: LCSH: Indians of North America--Juvenile literature. | Indians of North America--Social life and customs--Juvenile literature. | Indian mythology--North America--Juvenile literature. | Indians of North America--Folklore--Juvenile literature.
Classification: DDC 979--dc23
LC record available at http://lccn.loc.gov/2017930247

CONTENTS

NATIONS OF THE GREAT BASIN AND PLATEAU

I t is winter in the village. The family gathers around a fire in the evening. The warmth of the fire keeps the chill of the night air away. The children move close to their grandfather. He is about to tell a story. What will he tell tonight? The story begins.

Native American tribes have lived in the Great Basin and Plateau regions of the United States for thousands of years. They settled in an area that stretches across present-day

Members of the Southern Ute tribe prepare to perform a traditional dance in the winter.

MAP OF GREAT BASIN AND PLATEAU NATIONS

Several Native American Nations live in the Great Basin and Plateau regions of the United States. How do you think where each tribe mainly lived affected their way of life? How might that have had an impact on their oral traditions?

Washington, Idaho, Utah, Oregon, Montana, Nevada, Arizona, California, Wyoming, and Colorado. The Great Basin and Plateau regions have high deserts and low valleys. There are tall mountains, lakes, and rivers.

Several tribes live in the Great Basin. They include the Shoshone (Newe), the Paiute (Numa), and the Ute (Nuciu) tribes. The tribes of the Plateau region include the Nez Percé (Nimi'ipuu) and Yakama (Waptailmim).

HUNTING, FISHING, AND GATHERING

For thousands of years, the people of the Great Basin and Plateau regions survived by hunting and gathering their food. They hunted deer, elk, bison, antelope, moose, and caribou. They also hunted smaller animals such as jackrabbits and waterfowl.

The people used the skins and furs of the animals to make clothes, robes, and blankets. They used animal bones to make tools. They fished in rivers, lakes, and streams. They caught salmon, trout, and sturgeon.

The Great Basin and Plateau regions include both lush forests and arid deserts.

The people also gathered roots, berries, and nuts. They gathered food from the spring to the fall. Then they prepared and stored it to eat throughout the year.

Before contact with Europeans, the people living in the Great Basin and Plateau regions often moved with the seasons to follow food sources. They traveled in small groups and commonly settled near water.

BELIEFS AND STORYTELLING

Many people in the Great Basin and Plateau nations believe that everything in nature has a spirit, including animals, plants, and trees. They also believe that people are linked to the world around them. It is important to

stay in harmony with nature. Respecting nature strengthens the connection with these spirits.

Before Europeans arrived in America, Native Americans in the Great Basin and Plateau did not use a written language. Instead, they passed

PERSPECTIVES
A TIME FOR TALES
The Great Basin and Plateau people usually told stories only during the sacred winter season. The stories were often shared as a dramatic performance. The narrator would use different voices for each character. He or she would use gestures to emphasize different points of the story. The audience would also be involved, giving responses at different times.

Many members of Great Basin and Plateau Nations carry their traditions into the modern era.

on their history and culture through spoken storytelling. Storytelling was used for both entertainment and education. People told stories around the fire in the evening. A small group of family members and friends gathered. Food, such as dried deer or elk meat, would be passed around.

Similar to many other cultures, the Great Basin and Plateau tribes made sense of their world through storytelling. They used stories to explain nature and how the world was created. The people also created stories about the environment and problems facing the tribe.

The tribes used stories to record their history and culture. Some stories explained a tribe's customs and religious rituals. Other stories taught the values and ideals that were important to the tribe. The people passed these stories down from generation to generation. For these Native American nations, storytelling is a link from the past to the present.

THE WATER BABY

Many stories told by the Great Basin people featured the water baby. The water baby was an evil spirit. It lived in streams, lakes, and springs. In the stories, the water baby visited camps at night. Sometimes the evil spirit stole babies. Other times it mimicked the sound of a crying baby. Its cry pulled humans into the river at night, leading them to a watery grave. In many Great Basin and Plateau tribes, the cry of the water baby is considered to be an omen of death.

HUMAN CREATION

Native peoples in the Great Basin and Plateau regions have traditional creation stories. Coyote is an important figure in many stories from the Great Basin and Plateau cultures. In some stories, Coyote is a trickster. In other legends, he explains the natural world. The following is a Nez Percé creation story. In this story, Coyote creates people.

COYOTE CREATES HUMAN BEINGS

One day, before there were people on Earth, a great monster came from the North. He ate all of the animals, from the smallest to

Coyotes play a role in many traditional Native American stories.

the largest. Coyote could not find his friends. This made him mad. He decided to stop the monster.

Coyote crossed a river. He tied himself to the tallest peak of the mountains. Then he called to the monster. He dared the monster to cross the river and try to eat him. The monster charged across the river and climbed the mountain. He tried to suck Coyote off the mountain with his breath. But Coyote's rope was too strong. The monster decided to make friends with Coyote. He invited Coyote to come down from the mountain and stay with him.

One day Coyote told the monster that he would like to see the animals in the monster's belly. The monster agreed. When Coyote went inside, he saw that the animals were safe. Then Coyote built a large fire in the monster's belly. He used his knife to cut out the monster's heart. The monster died, and all the animals escaped. Coyote came out last.

In honor of the event, Coyote said that he was going to create a new animal called a human being. Coyote cut up the monster into pieces. He threw the pieces to the four winds. Some pieces landed in the North. Others landed in the South, West, and East. In each place a piece landed, a tribe was born. In this way, all the tribes came to be.

After he had finished, Fox told Coyote that there was no tribe where they stood. There were no more pieces of the monster left. So Coyote washed the blood from his paws and sprinkled the drops on the ground. From these drops, the Nez Percé tribe was born. Coyote said that they would be few in number but strong and pure.

CONFLICT OVER LAND

In the 1870s, the Nez Percé came into conflict with American settlers over their land. The settlers wanted the Nez Percé to move to a reservation and give up their land in Idaho and Oregon. Some Nez Percé agreed to go. Others refused. They were desperate to keep their sacred homelands. Several battles broke out between Nez Percé people and the US Army in 1877. The final battle occurred at Bear Paw Mountain in the Montana Territory in October. The Nez Percé surrendered. They were sent to a reservation in Idaho.

HOMELANDS OF THE NEZ PERCÉ

The Nez Percé live in the Pacific Northwest. They live in an area that covers parts of Washington, Oregon, and Idaho. Unlike some other Native American tribes, the Nez Percé do not have migration stories. Instead, their stories show them being present in their homeland since the creation of humans.

The Coyote creation story explains how humans came into the world. It also explains why the Nez Percé live where they do. In telling this story, the Nez Percé show how their homeland is sacred and important to them. They believe their tribe is special. They also believe they are meant to live on their homeland.

EXPLORE ONLINE

Chapter Two tells a story that features Coyote, a common character in many stories of the Great Basin and Plateau tribes. The website below explores other Coyote stories. As you know, every source is different. What information does the website give about Coyote stories from this region? How do these stories give you more information about the Great Basin and Plateau tribes?

LEGENDARY NATIVE AMERICAN FIGURES: COYOTE
abdocorelibrary.com/great-basin-and-plateau-nations

RESPECTING NATURE

Many Native American cultures have a deep knowledge of and respect for nature. They believe that all parts of nature are a precious gift from the Creator. By caring for nature and using its resources in a responsible way, the people show their appreciation for this gift. The following is a story from the Yakama people of Washington State. In this story, the people learn what happens if they do not take care of the salmon.

Yakama fisher Michael Andy pulls his catch from his net.

BIG TREES

The Paiute people traditionally lived across an area that includes parts of Oregon, Utah, Nevada, Arizona, and California. Like many other tribes, the Paiute teach respect for nature. In one story, they call the California big trees *woh-woh'-nau*. The word is formed to imitate an owl's hoot. According to the story, bad luck comes to those who cut down the big trees. Bad luck also comes to those who shoot an owl or shoot in an owl's presence. When American settlers came into Paiute land, the people tried to warn them not to cut down the big trees. When the settlers cut down the trees, the Paiute called after them. They told them that the owl would bring about evil.

LEGEND OF THE LOST SALMON

The Creator taught people how to care for the salmon. He told them not to take more than they needed. If they followed the rules, the salmon would be plentiful as long as the people lived. At first the people followed the Creator's rules. They lived happily in fishing villages along the river. They caught and dried the salmon.

One day, the people became

Nez Percé tribal member Brian J. Pinkham uses a traditional method to catch salmon.

careless and greedy. They caught more than they needed to feed their families. The salmon disappeared from the river. Soon the people became hungry. While searching the river, the people found a dead salmon on the river's bank. They cried in shame and felt sorry for their mistakes. The people called a council and tried to give life back to the salmon. Nothing worked.

LIFE CYCLE OF SALMON

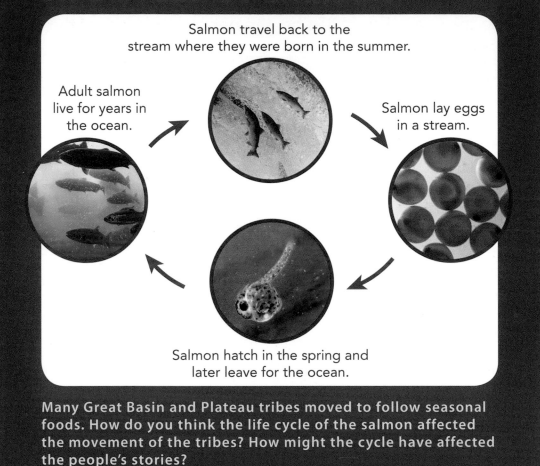

Salmon travel back to the stream where they were born in the summer.

Adult salmon live for years in the ocean.

Salmon lay eggs in a stream.

Salmon hatch in the spring and later leave for the ocean.

Many Great Basin and Plateau tribes moved to follow seasonal foods. How do you think the life cycle of the salmon affected the movement of the tribes? How might the cycle have affected the people's stories?

Desperate, the people called for Old Man Rattlesnake, who usually kept to himself. They asked him to help. Old Man Rattlesnake slowly crawled over the salmon four times. On the fifth time, Old Man Rattlesnake disappeared into the salmon. The salmon woke up and came back to life. Other salmon returned to the rivers. From then on, the people took care of the salmon and did not take more than they needed.

Today, when the people break open the salmon's spine, they find a white membrane. The membrane is said to be from Old Man Rattlesnake, who gave life to the salmon.

THE IMPORTANCE OF SALMON

The Yakama people are one of the Plateau Native nations. They live in the modern-day state of Washington, in the Columbia River Basin. The Yakama once moved with the seasons. Like many tribes in the Northwest, the Yakama depended on salmon as an important food source. In the spring, the Yakama moved close to the rivers. Many gathered at Celilo Falls, a major fishing and trade center. They caught salmon and preserved it. They managed how much they caught to make sure that there would be enough salmon each year.

DALLES DAM DESTROYS CELILO FALLS

In the early 1950s, the US Army Corps of Engineers started building the Dalles Dam. The dam spanned the Columbia River. On March 10, 1957, the dam was finished, and its steel gates crashed shut. The Columbia River was forced back, flooding all in its path. Within hours, the ancient Yakama fishing village of Celilo Falls was flooded. Tribes had come for thousands of years to fish and trade at Celilo Falls. The traditional tribal fishing site was lost.

The Yakama and other Great Basin and Plateau tribes show the importance of salmon by holding special rituals. They celebrate the return of the first fish with salmon ceremonies. The ceremonies have traditionally been held to ensure salmon would be plentiful for the year. Stories encouraged the people to limit how much they caught.

STRAIGHT TO THE
SOURCE

Corbin Harney was a Shoshone storyteller. In an interview, he talked about the role of the storyteller to educate people to respect nature:

> *My people always have said to me from the beginning of my life, as I remember . . . to take care of what's out here, what's out there on the land. All those things, we have to have ceremonies for. Those are the reasons why I've been trying to teach my people, not only my people, but the people that survive on all this land. To teach them we have to really start talking to the nature. [That] is the only way we are going to survive here.*

> Source: "Corbin Harney." *Circle of Stories*. PBS, n.d. Web. Accessed February 17, 2017.

Point of View

The author of this passage is a storyteller, and he has an opinion on how stories should be used. What is his point of view? What reasons does he give for this view?

EXPLAINING THE STARS IN THE SKY

The tribes of the Great Basin and Plateau regions use stories to explain the natural world. In many stories, the stars, sun, and moon are living beings and have humanlike qualities. The following is a Paiute legend. It explains how the North Star came to be and why it does not move in the night sky.

WHY THE NORTH STAR STANDS STILL

Long ago, when the North Star was on Earth, he was known as Na-gah, a mountain sheep.

In time-lapse photos, other stars appear to circle the North Star as it remains nearly still.

COYOTE PLACES THE STARS

In a story from the Wasco, Coyote places the stars in the sky. Coyote shot several arrows into the sky, one after another. They created a ladder to the sky. Coyote climbed the ladder with five wolf brothers. When they reached the sky, they found two bears. Coyote left them and climbed back to Earth. He took out the arrows so that no one could follow him. The wolves and bears became the constellation called the Big Dipper. The three oldest wolves make up the handle. The two youngest wolves and the bears make up the bowl under the handle. Coyote liked the way they looked so much that he arranged other stars in pictures across the sky.

He was brave, daring, and sure-footed. Every day, Na-gah hunted for the highest mountains and climbed.

Once, Na-gah found a very high peak that soared into the clouds. It had steep, smooth sides. Na-gah wanted to know what was at the top. He circled the mountain but could not find a trail. There were only sheer cliffs all around. He tried to climb, but each time he had to turn around and come down. Finally, Na-gah found a big crack in a rock that went down, not up. He went down into the crack. Inside, he found a hole that turned upward. He climbed up and up.

Soon it became dark and Na-gah could not see. Na-gah slipped often on loose rocks in the darkness. His courage faltered. "I will go back and look again for a better place to climb," he said to himself. "I am not afraid out on the open cliffs, but this dark hole fills me with fear. I'm scared! I want to get out of here!"

But Na-gah could not go back down. The rolling rocks had closed the cave below him. He could only keep climbing. After some time, Na-gah saw light. He climbed out of the hole and looked around. He was on the top of the highest peak, with Earth far below. He saw great cliffs below him in every direction. There was only a small space for him to move. He could not climb down the sheer cliffs, and the inside of the mountain was blocked. "Here I must stay until I die," he said.

"But I have climbed my mountain! I have climbed my mountain at last!"

Na-gah's father, Shinoh, called for his son. Na-gah answered his father from the top of the mountain. When Shinoh saw him, he felt sad. His brave son would not be able to come down. "I will not let my brave son die. I will turn him into a star, and he can stand there and shine where everyone can see him.

PAIUTE SHELTERS

Because they moved from place to place, the Paiute people lived in temporary shelters during the summer. They built windbreaks or small huts covered with rushes or bunches of local grasses. During the winter, they built more permanent cone-shaped shelters called wickiups. Wickiups had a frame of willow branches covered with reeds, brush, and grass. A hole at the top of the wickiup roof allowed smoke to escape. Rocks piled around the base of the hut provided more insulation from the cold. The people also added bark and earth to the wickiup for insulation.

Mountain sheep, also known as bighorn sheep, are found in many places throughout the Great Basin and Plateau regions.

He shall be a guide mark for all the living things on the earth or in the sky." In this way Na-gah became a star that every living thing can see. He became known as Qui-am-i Wintook Poot-see.

Other mountain sheep saw Na-gah at the top of the highest peak. They wanted to join him in the sky. Shinoh turned them into stars. They became constellations. They travel around the mountain, always trying to find the trail that leads up to Na-gah.

USING THE STARS AS A GUIDE

The Paiute people survived primarily by hunting and gathering. They hunted rabbits, deer, and mountain sheep. They gathered seasonal plants. The Paiute moved from place to place, following the supply of food.

For the Paiute people, the North Star was an important landmark. Because it does not move in the sky, people used it to find their way as they moved from place to place. Hunters used the position of the sun and the stars in the sky to find a specific landmark or to return to camp. Gatherers used the positions of the sun and stars to help them remember the locations of edible plants and water in the desert climate. Like other Native Americans and many cultures around the world, the Paiute also used the location of stars and constellations to signal seasons and events.

FURTHER EVIDENCE

Chapter Four discusses how stories are used to explain and explore the night sky. Explore the website below to learn about the many other uses for stories. Find a quote from the website that relates to something you read in the chapter. Does the quote support an existing piece of evidence in the chapter? Or does it add a new piece of evidence?

PBS: MANY VOICES
abdocorelibrary.com/great-basin-and-plateau-nations

THE LASTING IMPACT OF ORAL HISTORIES

In the 1800s, American settlers moved farther west into the lands of the Great Basin and Plateau people. Some tribes resisted giving up their land. They fought back against the invaders. Eventually, the US government removed many of the Great Basin and Plateau tribes from their territories. It forced them onto reservations throughout the region. They were forced to abandon their hunting and gathering lifestyle. The US

Nez Percé US park ranger Otis Halfmoon kneels near a historic battle site from one of the Nez Percé's conflicts with the US government.

PERSPECTIVES
DAMAGE TO THE LAND

As the settlers moved west, they caused irreparable harm to the land that had supported the Great Basin and Plateau people for thousands of years. The settlers set up farms on land rich in natural resources. They diverted water sources to irrigate their lands. And they banned traditional tribal methods of managing grasslands, such as regular burnings. The settlers also brought livestock with them. The horses and cattle compacted the soil and overgrazed, ruining the seed grasses. With a dwindling space and food supply, native animals disappeared. The land could no longer support the tribes.

government outlawed parts of traditional culture. Throughout these hardships and challenges, the Great Basin and Plateau Nations worked hard to keep their cultures alive.

Today, members of the Great Basin and Plateau Nations live in many areas of the country. Some live in tribal communities in the Northwest. Others live in cities and towns elsewhere in the United States. To preserve their culture and traditions, the tribes hold festivals and annual celebrations. They teach Native languages and history in schools.

Oral traditions and storytelling also keep Native American cultures and history alive. In addition, some people have begun to write down stories. These written records are another way to preserve the traditions of the Great Basin and Plateau people.

STORYTELLING TODAY

Like many Native American tribes, the people of the Great Basin and Plateau have an extensive oral history. Their

PROTECTING TRIBAL CULTURE

In addition to storytelling, people are working to preserve tribal culture in other ways. The Museum at Warm Springs preserves the culture, history, and traditions of the Confederated Tribes of Warm Springs, which are part of the Plateau region. This group includes the Warm Springs, Wasco, and Paiute tribes. The museum holds tribal artifacts. It also features exhibits to educate visitors about the Warm Springs tribes.

oral traditions include stories, songs, and orations. For centuries, the people of the Great Basin and Plateau passed down their history by word of mouth. In oral traditions, they recorded the details of important events, daily life, and religious rituals and ceremonies.

Storytelling remains important to the Great Basin and Plateau people. The Paiute and other tribes still tell stories to entertain and teach morals. They tell stories to keep tribal history and culture alive. Myrtle Peck, a member of the Paiute Nation, says her mother often told her stories about the trickster Coyote and other animals. As she grew older, Peck's mother told her stories about the family's history. She described life for Northern Paiute people when they traveled from place to place. Today, Peck shares these Paiute stories with her own daughter. Peck's daughter wants to pass the stories on to her own children, nieces, and nephews.

Storytellers from Washington perform for children in Europe, sharing their traditions with a global audience.

Tribal members such as Leroy Spotted Eagle have maintained Paiute traditions over the years.

By doing so, she hopes to keep the heritage of the Paiute people alive.

The stories told today have been passed down from generation to generation. These stories are a window to the past. They help people today learn more about the beliefs, cultures, and history of the Great Basin and Plateau Nations.

STRAIGHT TO THE
SOURCE

Vinton Hawley is the chairman of the Pyramid Lake Paiute Tribe in Nevada. When asked about his responsibilities, he responded:

> *It is my responsibility to make decisions that ensure our way of life continues. . . . To ensure that our tribal language and traditions are sustained is my priority. . . .*
>
> *I continue to advocate for the sustainability of the Paiute culture. However, despite my position, culture is not funded by the tribe, nor do we have a grant to assist cultural sustainability. Tribal members in our community volunteer to maintain the culture and have classes on a weekly basis. I have to give high praise to those individuals who are as passionate about cultural preservation as I am.*

Source: "Meet Native America: Vinton Hawley." *National Museum of the American Indian*. NMAI, November 1, 2016. Web. Accessed January 30, 2017.

What's the Big Idea?

Take a close look at Hawley's words. What is his main idea? What evidence does he use to support his point?

STORY
SUMMARIES

Coyote Creates Human Beings (Nez Percé)

Before there are people, a great monster eats all of the animals. Coyote goes inside the monster's belly to find his friends. He kills the monster and frees the animals. He cuts the monster into pieces. He scatters the pieces to the North, South, East, and West. In each place where a piece lands, a tribe is born. Then Coyote washes the blood from his hands and sprinkles it on the ground where he stands. From these drops the Nez Percé tribe is born.

Legend of the Lost Salmon (Yakama)

The Creator teaches the people how to care for salmon. But the people become greedy. They take more salmon than they need. The salmon disappear, and the people go hungry. They find a dead salmon on the riverbank. No one can revive it. The people ask Old Man Rattlesnake for help. He crawls over the salmon four times. On the fifth time, he disappears into the salmon. The salmon comes back to life. Other salmon return to the rivers. The people learn their lesson and take care of the salmon.

Why the North Star Stands Still (Paiute)

Na-gah is a mountain sheep that likes to climb to the highest peak of the mountains. One day he finds a peak that soars into the highest clouds. After much searching, he climbs to the top and looks down upon Earth. Once there, Na-gah cannot climb down. His father Shinoh turns Na-gah into a star. He becomes the North Star, which is a guide for all living things on Earth. Other mountain sheep try to join Na-gah on the mountain peak. Shinoh turns them into stars. They travel around the mountain, always trying to find the trail that leads to Na-gah.

STOP AND
THINK

Say What?

Find five words in this book that you are unfamiliar with. Find each word in the glossary or a dictionary. Rewrite each word's definition in your own words. Then use each word in a new sentence.

Why Do I Care?

Think about how stories and oral traditions play a part in your own life. What kinds of stories do you hear and see? How are stories that you hear in person different from those you experience over the Internet or on television?

Another View

Find another source about the Great Basin and Plateau peoples. Write a short essay comparing and contrasting its point of view with that of this book's author. Be sure to answer these questions: What is the point of view of each author? How are they similar and why? How are they different and why?

Surprise Me

Think about what you learned from this book. What two or three facts did you find most surprising? Write a short paragraph about each, describing what you found surprising and why.

GLOSSARY

ceremonies
formal events that are celebrated by many people

council
a group of people who manage the affairs of a village, city, or town

culture
the shared ways of life and beliefs of a group of people

oral traditions
stories, songs, and speeches that are passed from generation to generation by word of mouth

plateau
an area of relatively level high ground

rituals
religious or solemn ceremonies consisting of a series of actions performed according to a prescribed order

sacred
something that is respected or believed to be holy

tribe
a group of Native people who share a common culture and language

windbreaks
structures that provide shelter or protection from wind

LEARN MORE

Books

Powell, Marie. *Traditional Stories of the Plains Nations.* Minneapolis, MN: Abdo Publishing, 2018.

Treuer, Anton. *Atlas of Indian Nations.* Washington, DC: National Geographic, 2013.

Yasuda, Anita. *Traditional Stories of the Northwest Coast Nations.* Minneapolis, MN: Abdo Publishing, 2018.

Websites

To learn more about Native American Oral Histories, visit **abdobooklinks.com**. These links are routinely monitored and updated to provide the most current information available.

Visit **abdocorelibrary.com** for free additional tools for teachers and students.

INDEX

About the Author

Carla Mooney is the author of several books for young readers. She loves learning about people, places, and events in history. A graduate of the University of Pennsylvania, she lives in Pittsburgh, Pennsylvania, with her husband and three children.